ASTRID & APOLLO

AND THE
FISHING FLOP

BY
V.T. BIDANIA

ILLUSTRATED BY
DARA LASHIA LEE

PICTURE WINDOW BOOKS
a capstone imprint

P9-CLA-907

To Mahal, who took me fishing. — V.T.B.

Astrid and Apollo is published by Picture Window Books,
an imprint of Capstone.
1710 Roe Crest Drive
North Mankato, Minnesota 56003
www.capstonepub.com

Text copyright © 2021 by V.T. Bidania.
Illustrations copyright © 2021 by Capstone.

All rights reserved. No part of this publication may be reproduced in whole or in
part, or stored in a retrieval system, or transmitted in any form or by any means,
electronic, mechanical, photocopying, recording, or otherwise, without written
permission of the publisher.

Library of Congress Cataloging-in-Publication Data
Names: Bidania, V. T., author. | Lee, Dara Lashia, illustrator.
Title: Astrid and Apollo and the fishing flop / by V.T. Bidania ;
    illustrated by Dara Lashia Lee.
Description: North Mankato, Minnesota : Picture Window Books, an imprint of
    Capstone, [2020] | Series: Astrid and Apollo | Audience: Ages 6-8. |
    Summary: Hmong-American twins Astrid and Apollo are on their very first
    fishing trip, but while Astrid catches three fine fish, Apollo's line
    keeps snagging on non-fish things, and when a summer storm brings the
    trip to a sudden end Apollo admits he is disappointed with the
    experience—until he gets a look at the funny pictures their dad has
    taken.
Identifiers: LCCN 2019058187 (print) | LCCN 2019058188 (ebook) | ISBN
    9781515861232 (hardcover) | ISBN 9781515861270 (paperback) | ISBN
    9781515861287 (adobe pdf)
Subjects: LCSH: Hmong American children—Juvenile fiction. | Hmong American
    families—Juvenile fiction. | Twins—Juvenile fiction. | Brothers and
    sisters—Juvenile fiction. | Fishing stories. | CYAC: Hmong
    Americans—Fiction. | Twins—Fiction. | Brothers and sisters—Fiction. |
    Fishing—Fiction.
Classification: LCC PZ7.1.B5333 An 2020 (print) | LCC PZ7.1.B5333 (ebook)
    | DDC [Fic]—dc23
LC record available at https://lccn.loc.gov/201905818
LC ebook record available at https://lccn.loc.gov/2019058188

Designer: Lori Bye

Design Elements: Shutterstock: Ingo Menhard, Yangxiong

Printed and bound in the United States of America.   PO3818

R0458782383

Table of Contents

Hi, I'm Astrid. My twin brother is Apollo, and we were born in Minnesota. We live here with our mom, dad, and little sister, Eliana.

ASTRID GAO NOU

Hi, I'm Apollo! Our mom and dad were both born in Laos. They came to the United States when they were very young and grew up here.

APOLLO NOU KOU

MOM, DAD, AND ELIANA GAO CHEE

HMONG WORDS

gao (GOW)—girl; it is often placed in front of a girl's name. Hmong spelling: *nkauj*

Gao Chee (GOW chee)—shiny girl. Hmong spelling: *Nkauj Ci*

Gao Nou (GOW new)—sun girl. Hmong spelling: *Nkauj Hnub*

Hmong (MONG)—a group of people who came to the U.S. from Laos. Many Hmong from Laos now live in Minnesota. Hmong spelling: *Hmoob*

Nou Kou (NEW koo)—star. Hmong spelling: *Hnub Qub*

tou (TOO)—boy or son; it is often placed in front of a boy's name. Hmong spelling: *tub*

CHAPTER 1

Tickle Box

"Over here! Kick it this way!" said Apollo.

Astrid kicked the soccer ball toward him, but it missed Apollo. The ball bounced on the ground and rolled into the garage.

"I'll get it!" said Apollo.

The sun shined on his face as he chased the ball.

The wind blew at the trees, shaking the branches. It was a warm and windy day.

As Apollo ran after the ball, he didn't see the thin white wire on the garage floor. His shoe got stuck in the wire. Apollo tripped and fell down.

"Hey!" he said.

Astrid came running. "What happened?" she asked. "Are you okay?"

Apollo sat up. The wire was wrapped around his ankle.

"What's that?" said Astrid.

Dad hurried over from where he was cleaning the car.

"Are you all right?" he said.

Apollo nodded.

Astrid showed the wire to Dad. "This tripped him!"

"You found my line," said Dad. He helped Apollo unwrap the line and pulled him up. "I'm sorry. That fell out of the car."

"What's it for?" said Apollo.

"I'll show you," Dad said.

Astrid and Apollo followed him to the back of the car.

Dad held up the line. "Twins, take a good look."

They looked closer at the line. Then they looked inside the car trunk. They saw a plastic box with a handle. It looked like a toolbox.

Astrid pointed at the box. "What's that called again? Is it a tickle box?"

Apollo suddenly remembered. "It's a tackle box!"

"Yes! Tomorrow I'm taking you fishing," said Dad.

"Thanks, Dad!" Astrid said happily.

"We've wanted to go fishing for so long!" said Apollo.

Dad smiled. "Remember? We had to wait for fishing season to open. It starts tomorrow. The weather should be perfect."

"We can use the fishing poles we got for Christmas," said Astrid.

"Finally!" said Apollo.

Mom and Dad had given them fishing poles for Christmas. Astrid got a shiny green pole. Apollo got a bright blue pole.

"Get to bed on time tonight. We're leaving early in the morning," Dad said.

"Now we can learn how to fish! We can take pictures holding a fish too," said Apollo.

Dad nodded. "Yes!"

Apollo had seen pictures of his cousins fishing. In each picture, they held up the big fish they caught. They smiled the happiest smiles.

Now it was his turn. Apollo couldn't wait to take pictures with all the big fish he would catch! He liked making people laugh. He would make sure to smile a happy smile. He would make sure his pictures were funny and silly.

Just then, the wind blew again. The fishing line fell to the ground. Astrid and Apollo chased the line down the sunny driveway.

* * *

Apollo was still sleeping when a light shined under his bedroom door. It woke him up. He turned to the clock by his bed. It was 5:00 in the morning!

The door opened. Dad was in the hallway. "Time to get up!"

Apollo hid his face under the pillow. "It's so early."

"We want to get to the lake before the sun rises. That's when the fish start biting. Did I tell you we get to ride in Uncle Lue's boat?" Dad said.

Apollo sat up. "Really?"

Uncle Lue had a big, fast boat he used for fishing every summer. Apollo and Astrid always wanted to ride in the boat, but they'd never had a chance.

"Yes," said Dad. "Now please wake up your sister. I'll go finish packing supplies."

Apollo hopped out of bed. He ran across the hall to Astrid's room. He knocked on the door and said, "Astrid?"

"Come in," she said sleepily.

Apollo pushed open the door. "Get up! Dad's taking us fishing now."

Astrid yawned. "Why so early?"

"We have to get there before sunrise. Dad said we get to ride in Uncle Lue's boat!"

Astrid's eyes opened wide. "His big, fast boat?"

"Yes!" said Apollo.

"Yay!" said Astrid.

CHAPTER 2

Big and Juicy

When Apollo got to the kitchen, he smelled eggs and bacon. A pot of chicken in lemongrass was boiling next to the pan. Behind that, steam came out of the rice cooker.

Mom was by the stove. "Good morning," she said.

"Good morning! Where's Dad?" said Apollo.

Mom pointed to the side door with a big spoon. "He's in the garage."

"Thanks." Apollo smiled a big, happy smile. "Mom, I'll be smiling like this for pictures I take with the fish. They'll be the goofiest pictures in the world!"

"I can't wait to see them!" said Mom.

Apollo grabbed a piece of bacon, put on his shoes, and stepped into the garage.

Dad was putting life vests in the car.

Apollo saw the fishing poles on top of the car. "Dad, don't forget those!"

"Thanks! We can't fish without these." Dad set them in the car.

Mom and Astrid came out with bags of food.

"Here are bacon and egg sandwiches for breakfast, and boiled chicken and rice for lunch," said Mom.

"And coconut juice and jelly cups for fun," said Astrid.

"Thank you!" Dad said.

"What else do we need?" Apollo asked.

"There's one last thing we need, but we will pick it up with Uncle Lue. Now it's time to go!" said Dad.

The twins and Dad got into the car.

As Dad drove out of the garage, Astrid and Apollo looked out the car window. It was still dark outside.

Mom stood by the front door carrying Eliana.

Astrid opened the window. "Bye, Eliana."

"I'll take funny pictures for you," said Apollo.

Eliana kept her head on Mom's shoulder. She looked sad, like she wanted to go, but Mom said she was too young to fish all day.

"Have fun," Mom said. "Bring back some fish for dinner!"

"We will, Mom!" said Astrid.

"We'll bring back the biggest fish you ever saw!" said Apollo.

Mom smiled. "As long as you have fun, that's all that counts."

* * *

When they got to Uncle Lue's house, they saw his big truck parked in front. The boat was behind the truck, shining under the streetlight. It was even bigger than the truck.

Uncle Lue was wiping the side of the boat.

"Hi, Uncle Lue!" Apollo said when they got out of the car.

"Your boat looks so shiny!" said Astrid.

Uncle Lue laughed. "Hi, kids! You have to wipe it to keep the shine. Now who wants to go fishing?"

Dad and Uncle Lue packed the fishing supplies into the boat. They tied everything down. Astrid and Apollo climbed into the back seats of the truck. Dad and Uncle Lue sat in the front.

Apollo was looking forward to the boat ride. "How fast is your boat, Uncle Lue?" he asked.

"It's fast, but with kids on board, I promise not to go too fast," said Uncle Lue.

Apollo frowned at Astrid. She frowned back. They wanted to go fast.

Then Uncle Lue drove to a small store by the gas station. "I'll be right back!" he said.

When he came back, he said, "I got our bait."

Astrid looked at the container he was holding. "Are those worms?" she asked.

Apollo read the words *NIGHT CRAWLERS* on the container. "They are!" he said.

"Not just any worms. These are special. They're big and juicy," said Uncle Lue.

Apollo grinned.

"I don't want to touch them!" Astrid said.

Apollo didn't want to touch the worms either. But he wanted to catch fish. "I'll do it," he said.

Dad smiled. "They're not so bad. I'll show you how to put them on the fish hook."

Astrid shook her head. "No way!"

Dad, Apollo, and Uncle Lue laughed. Astrid couldn't help but laugh too.

As Uncle Lue drove out of the city, Astrid and Apollo ate the bacon and egg sandwiches. As they passed small towns, big farms, and huge parks, they drank coconut juice.

Finally, they reached a large lake.

The sun was rising. The sky turned a light blue color.

Dad pointed up ahead. "There it is, twins. That's where we'll be fishing."

Astrid and Apollo stared at the lake. It was so big. The water looked pretty under the sunrise.

"Time to launch the boat!" said Uncle Lue. He backed up the truck until the boat was in the water.

Dad unhooked the boat from the truck and tied it to the dock.

After Uncle Lue left to park the truck, Dad passed out life vests. "We need to always wear these when on the boat or dock," he said.

Suddenly the wind blew so hard, Astrid's hair flew in the air. It hit Apollo's face.

"It sure is windy this morning!" Dad said.

Then Uncle Lue came back and climbed into the boat. "Get in, kids!"

Dad helped Astrid and Apollo get into the boat before he hopped in. The boat wobbled in the water.

As everyone sat in their seats, Apollo looked out at the lake. "This is so cool!"

Dad untied the boat from the dock. Uncle Lue turned on the motor.

"All right, everybody. Let's go!" he said.

CHAPTER 3

How Much Longer?

The boat zoomed forward. Water sprayed up the sides. Tiny drops fell on Astrid's and Apollo's arms.

"This is so fun!" Astrid laughed.

Apollo nodded. "It's really fun!"

"Hold on tight!" Uncle Lue steered the boat to the side. Astrid and Apollo held on to their seats as they leaned to the side.

The sun was up now. The boat moved along, faster and faster.

Waves rose up and down. The boat went right over the waves. The wind blew at their faces.

"I wish we could do this every day!" said Apollo.

"Me too!" said Astrid.

When they were close to the middle of the lake, Uncle Lue slowed down. The boat motor grew quiet.

"Now we can fish," Dad said.

He handed out the fishing poles and gave Astrid and Apollo each a pair of gloves.

"When you hold a fish," Dad said, "be sure to wear gloves to protect your hands. But first it's time for bait."

"Do I have to use a night crawler?" Astrid said.

"Would you rather use lures?" Uncle Lue opened the tackle box. Inside were plastic and rubber minnows in bright colors.

"Oh, those little fish are so cute. Yes, please!" Astrid said.

Uncle Lue helped Astrid hang a pink and green minnow on her hook. Dad helped Apollo put a night crawler on his hook.

Apollo made a face. "My bait is so mushy!"

"So is mine!" said Astrid.

"But mine is real and yours is fake!" Apollo said.

Astrid laughed.

Dad showed them the parts of
the pole. "This is the rod, this is the
reel, and this is the bobber. This is
how you cast." He swung the pole to
the side and tossed the fishing line
into the water.

Astrid and Apollo watched the line fly into the lake. It dropped into the water and made a little splash.

Uncle Lue cast his line next.

"Now what?" said Apollo.

Uncle Lue sat on his seat. "Now you wait. If you see your bobber move, it means something bit your bait."

Astrid and Apollo cast their lines into the water, just the way Dad showed them. Then they waited.

A breeze blew over the water. Geese flew above them. The geese honked loud honks. Everything was very still.

"How much longer do we wait?" asked Apollo.

"When will they bite?" asked Astrid.

"You have to be patient," said Dad. "I'll show you how to cast it somewhere else if you want. Pull the line back in. That's called reeling."

Dad turned the handle on his reel. The line came back. He faced a different direction of the lake and cast it into the water again.

Apollo did the same thing. So did Astrid. Then they waited. Nothing happened, so they reeled and cast their lines once more.

The sun was so bright on top of the water. Apollo squinted.

"How much longer?" Astrid asked.

"Remember, be patient," said Dad.

Astrid looked at Apollo. Apollo shrugged. She shrugged back.

The sun shined down onto their heads. The air felt so hot. Astrid pushed her hair away from her face. Apollo rubbed the sweat off his nose.

It was relaxing on the lake. But when was he going to catch a big fish? Apollo was ready to take funny pictures.

Across the lake, he saw a family hiking by the trees. On the other side, people climbed into their boats by the dock. Another boat of fishers rode past their boat.

"Any bites?" a man on the other boat asked Apollo.

Apollo shook his head. "Not yet."

"Good luck," the man said as his
boat moved away.

"Thanks." Apollo cast his line
one more time. Suddenly he felt a
tug on the line. "I think I caught
something!"

CHAPTER 4

Stuck!

His first fish! Apollo was so excited.

He pulled the rod, but he couldn't reel the line back in.

"It must be a big one, Apollo!" said Uncle Lue.

Apollo pulled hard. And harder. And harder still. The line would not come out.

Then Astrid said, "Oh! I got something too! Uncle Lue, can you help me?"

Uncle Lue stood up to help Astrid.

Dad looked at Apollo. "You need some help?"

"I think I got it!" said Apollo. "Can you get ready to take a picture of me?"

Dad nodded. As Apollo pulled on his line, Uncle Lue helped Astrid with hers.

Apollo watched Astrid and Uncle Lue reel in a large fish. It flapped in the air.

"My first fish!" Astrid said.

"That's a nice-looking crappie!" said Uncle Lue.

"Dad, can you take pictures?" Astrid said.

Astrid held the crappie. Dad used the camera on his phone to take pictures. Astrid laughed as the fish flapped by her face.

Apollo couldn't wait to take pictures too. But he just could not get his line out. He pulled so hard that his pole bent forward. Then Apollo saw something under the water. The line was twisted in it.

Dad leaned over the side of the boat to look. "It's stuck in the weeds," he said.

"It's not a fish?" Apollo asked.

"Sorry. Let's get it out and try again," said Dad.

Dad yanked the line out and tried to pull off the weeds. "They won't come off," he said. "We have to cut the line."

"Sorry," said Apollo.

"Don't worry. It happens to all of us." Dad cut the line and put in a new hook and bobber. He handed the pole back to Apollo. Apollo hung another night crawler on the hook.

"Apollo, did you see the fish I got?" said Astrid.

Apollo nodded. "Good job, Astrid." Then he cast his line.

The wind blew again, harder this time. Apollo watched tree branches swinging in the distance.

Just then, Astrid said, "My bobber went under again!"

Uncle Lue helped Astrid reel her line back in. This fish looked bigger than the first one.

"Another crappie! It's big!" Uncle Lue said.

Dad took pictures of Astrid.

Astrid laughed as she posed. "Look, Apollo! I got a bigger one this time!"

"That's great," Apollo said. Suddenly he felt another tug. "I got one too!"

Something was pulling on his line. He tried to reel it in, but it felt heavy. Was his line stuck again?

Apollo pulled so hard. "Something is dragging it down," he said. "Dad, help!"

Dad put away his phone and helped Apollo pull. Together, they reeled in the line until Apollo saw something underwater.

It didn't look like a fish.

He turned the reel as hard as he could. Something was hanging from the line, but it wasn't a fish. It was someone's dirty old tennis shoe!

"It's a shoe!" he said.

"Sorry," Dad said.

As Dad helped Apollo untangle the shoe from the hook, the wind blew again. The clouds were now covering the sun.

"It sure got cloudy," Astrid said.

"It's getting dark," said Apollo.

Across the lake, he saw the family hiking turn around.

Dad looked up. "The news said we're supposed to have sunshine all day."

"The weather changed. Hopefully it won't rain," said Uncle Lue.

"Hope not," said Apollo, but he saw the waves around them getting bigger.

"I got another one!" Astrid suddenly said.

Uncle Lue helped Astrid again. "You're having a lot of luck today!"

Dad got out his camera phone one more time. "This is your third crappie!"

That's when Apollo saw his bobber disappear under the water. "I got something too!" he said. His line swung. He held on tight.

"Want help?" Dad said.

"I got it!" Apollo yanked the pole, but he couldn't get the line out.

Then he felt a drop of water on his arm. Soon another drop came. Then another. Was it raining?

Apollo pulled one last time.
A long, dark fish came up out of
the water. "Look!" he said happily.
Finally! Apollo felt so proud.

The fish flopped from side to
side, splashing water everywhere.
Apollo's arms hurt as he reeled it in.
He set the fish on the boat floor.

Suddenly more drops fell. Apollo looked up. It was raining!

The sky had turned gray with big, puffy clouds. The waves rose higher. The other boats that passed them earlier were turning around.

Apollo looked down at his fish. He looked at Astrid's fish that she was putting in the bucket. Her fish were round, but his fish was long. Its head had no scales.

"What'd you get?" Dad said.

"I don't know," said Apollo.

The fish's face looked a little scary. The body reminded him of an eel.

"That looks like a dogfish," said Dad.

Uncle Lou looked over. "It's a dogfish, all right. It's also called a bowfin."

Then thunder boomed. Rain poured down. Other boats zipped past them, heading to the dock. All of a sudden, lightning lit up the sky.

"We should get out of here! It's not safe to be on the water during a storm," said Uncle Lue. "Kids, hold on!"

Astrid and Apollo sat down. Uncle Lue turned the boat back toward the dock. The rain fell harder and harder. Uncle Lue went fast so the boat motor was loud. The rain was loud too.

"We're getting all wet!" Astrid said.

Apollo looked at the dogfish flopping by his feet. "Dad, what do I do?" He had to yell so Dad could hear.

"Sorry, Apollo! We don't usually keep dogfish!" said Dad.

"You can toss it back! We'll try for more crappies later, okay?" Uncle Lue said.

"Okay!" Apollo was disappointed, but he didn't want a dogfish.

Dad put on gloves and took the dogfish off the hook. Under the rain, he and Apollo picked it up and tossed it into the lake. It made a splash.

Lightning flashed again. Waves pushed the boat around. The tackle box and cooler slid to the side of the boat. Astrid fell from her seat and almost hit Apollo.

"I don't like this!" she cried.

"It's okay, Astrid!" Apollo said.

"Come here!" Dad said.

Astrid ran to hug Dad.

Apollo wiped the rain from his eyes. It was so windy and dark.

"Don't worry, kids! We're almost there!" Uncle Lue said.

Then thunder clapped again. Apollo jumped up and hugged Dad too.

Finally they reached the dock. Waves spilled inside the boat. Rain poured down as Dad helped Astrid and Apollo out of the boat. Uncle Lue ran to get the truck as Dad tied the boat to the dock.

The twins waited with Dad in the rain until Uncle Lue came back with the truck. Then they climbed inside. After Dad attached the boat to the truck, he got in the front seat. Uncle Lue drove away from the dock as more lightning flashed.

CHAPTER 5

Silly and Goofy

Astrid and Apollo sat in the truck and ate jelly cups as it rained. The truck was parked next to other cars in the parking lot. Every few minutes, thunder boomed. Astrid and Apollo jumped.

As they ate the jelly cups, Apollo watched rain slide down the truck windows. Astrid looked at pictures on Dad's phone.

"Kids, you did a great job fishing," Uncle Lue said.

"I got three in a row!" said Astrid.

Dad nodded. "They were big fish."

Apollo didn't say anything. He felt happy for Astrid, but he felt sorry for himself. He didn't catch anything big. He didn't even get to take pictures.

"Are you okay, Apollo? I'm sorry you didn't get to keep your fish. I know you'll catch more later," said Astrid.

"Thanks, but I want to go home," he said.

"What? Why?" said Astrid.

"You got three big fish, and I only got a dogfish. It wasn't even big," said Apollo.

Astrid put the phone down. "But we didn't come just to catch big fish. We came to learn *how* to fish. Anyway, Mom said it doesn't matter how big they are, remember? What counts is that we have fun."

Apollo thought about what Astrid said. He did have fun riding on the boat. He did like learning how to put a mushy night crawler on a hook, and how to cast and reel. "But I didn't take any funny pictures," he said.

Astrid looked at the phone again. "Look at this!" She showed him the first picture of her holding a fish. In the background, Apollo was pulling at the weeds. The look on his face was silly.

Apollo smiled.

"Look at this one!" said Astrid.

In the next picture, Apollo was behind Astrid, pulling at the shoe he caught. He had a funny, surprised look on his face.

Apollo laughed.

"Check out this one!" Astrid said.

Apollo saw his face in the last picture. He was staring at the dogfish. He looked silly, funny, and surprised.

Apollo laughed harder. "That is a funny picture!"

"That fish is *not* cute!" said Astrid.

Apollo shook his head as they laughed, ate more jelly cups, and looked at more pictures.

"Can you take a break from pictures and jelly cups for lunch?" Dad said. He passed them the chicken, soup, and rice. Astrid and Apollo ate the chicken in lemongrass soup with rice.

"This is so good!" said Astrid.

Apollo bit into a drumstick. "It's delicious."

Soon the rain stopped. The sky cleared. People were getting out of their cars and walking back to the dock.

"We can go back on the lake?" Apollo asked in surprise.

"Sure. The weather's better, so it's safe," said Uncle Lue.

"Let's finish lunch first," Dad said.

By the time they were done eating, it was sunny again. The lake looked calm. More people were getting into their boats.

"Should we go back out?" Uncle Lue said.

Dad turned around. "Twins, what do you say? More fishing?"

"Yes!" they said.

* * *

When they got home that evening, they had a cooler full of fish for Mom.

Mom smiled. "Crappies! My favorite fish to cook. And they are so big!"

"Mom, it doesn't matter how big they are," said Astrid.

"What counts is that we had fun!" Apollo said.

Mom nodded. "That's right! So you liked fishing? Apollo, did you take any silly pictures?"

Apollo showed Mom the funniest picture of all. "We sure did!" he said and grinned at Astrid.

- Hmong people first lived in southern China. Many of them moved to Southeast Asia in the 1800s. Some Hmong decided to stay in the country of Laos (pronounced *LAH-ohs*).

LAOS

- In the 1950s, a war called the Vietnam War started in Southeast Asia. The United States joined this war. They asked the Hmong in Laos to help them. When the U.S. lost the war, Hmong people had to leave Laos.

- After 1975, many Hmong came to the U.S. as refugees. Refugees are people who escape from their country to find a new, safe place to live. Today, Minnesota is home to around 85,000 Hmong.

- Many Hmong American families enjoy outdoor activities like camping, boating, and fishing.

chicken in lemongrass soup—chicken boiled in broth or soup with lemongrass. This is a popular Hmong dish that is often packed to be eaten on trips.

coconut juice—a drink made from the juice of young coconuts. Coconut juice comes in a can or a small box with a straw. This drink is enjoyed by many Hmong children.

crappie—a freshwater fish that is a favorite among Hmong fishers. Crappies can be fried or cooked in a stew with tomatoes, cilantro, and onions.

jelly cups—a sweet Asian jelly candy that comes in different flavors and colors. It is packaged in a small plastic cup. Jelly cups can be found in almost every Asian grocery store.

lemongrass—an herb that smells like lemon. It is used as a flavoring in many Hmong and Southeast Asian dishes.

bait (BAYT)—a small amount of food put on a hook to attract a fish

bobber (BOB-er)—something that floats on the surface of a fluid

cast (KAST)—to throw a fishing line into the water by using a fishing pole

dogfish (DAWG-fish)—a medium-sized freshwater fish found in lakes and streams

launch (LAWNCH)—to put a boat on the water

lure (LOOR)—fake bait used for catching fish

minnow (MIN-oh)—a small freshwater fish often used as bait

motor (MOH-tur)—a machine that provides the power to make something run or move

patient (PAY-shuhnt)—able to put up with problems without getting angry or upset

squint (SKWINT)—to look at something through partly closed eyes, especially when there is too much light

zoom (ZOOM)—to move quickly, with a loud humming sound

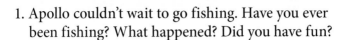

1. Apollo couldn't wait to go fishing. Have you ever been fishing? What happened? Did you have fun?

2. Apollo felt so disappointed he didn't catch a big fish. Discuss a time you felt disappointed when things didn't go the way you expected.

3. What did Astrid say to Apollo when he felt bad he didn't catch any big fish? Talk about a time when you had to cheer up a friend. What did you say to make them feel better?

WRITE IT DOWN

1. Have you ever ridden in a boat? What was it like? If not, have you ever ridden something that was very fast? Write a paragraph about it. Draw a picture of yourself in the fast boat or on the fast ride.

2. Astrid and Apollo felt nervous when the storm came. Pretend you are Astrid or Apollo and write a poem about being stuck in the rainstorm. Describe how you felt in the boat under the lightning and thunder.

3. Apollo wanted to take funny pictures of himself to make people laugh. Have you ever taken a goofy picture of yourself? Write about it and draw yourself making a funny face or doing a silly pose.

V.T. Bidania was born in Laos and grew up in St. Paul, Minnesota. She spent most of her childhood writing stories, and now that she's an adult, she is thrilled to be writing stories for children. She has an MFA in creative writing from The New School and is a recipient of the Loft Literary Center's Mirrors and Windows Fellowship. She lives outside of the Twin Cities with her family.

Dara Lashia Lee is a Hmong American illustrator based in the Twin Cities in Minnesota. She utilizes digital media to create semi-realistic illustrations ranging from Japanese anime to western cartoon styles. Her Hmong-inspired illustrations were displayed at the Qhia Dab Neeg (Storytelling) touring exhibit from 2015 to 2018. When she's not drawing, she likes to travel, take silly photos of her cat, and drink bubble tea.